MEET
WILL AND JAKE
Best Buds Forever

Written by Community Living Kincardine and District's Infant & Child Development Program, and the families of the Homies with Extra Chromies group.

Illustrated by Sarah Diebel

Tellwell Talent
www.tellwell.ca

ISBN
978-0-2288-0291-4 (Paperback)

This book is dedicated to the **Homies with Extra Chromies,** a group of preschoolers and their parents who are changing the conversation about inclusion in the town of Kincardine, Ontario, and challenging peoples' assumptions of what it means to have Down syndrome.

To Pippa, Austin, Logan and Kitaro, we know you have the power to change the world for the better, and to your friends Liam, Lukas, Lydia, Gage and all others who will come after you, joining your force for good.

A Note for Readers

Dear Reader,

In the spring of 2017, I had the opportunity to spend a few days in beautiful Kincardine, Ontario. I was the guest of Community Living Kincardine, and my purpose was to lead a series of conversations and training workshops about including children and youth with disabilities in all aspects of community life. In addition to finding Kincardine an utterly charming town, I also discovered that its residents were warm and welcoming.

It is not always easy to be welcoming to people who think, talk, move, or act differently than we do. It can be scary, and our fear can get in the way of the opportunity we have to build meaningful relationships with people who will add richness to our lives. We all benefit from widening our circle to include all kinds of people.

It is important that we help the children in our lives with understanding and appreciating human diversity. Their natural curiosity about the world around them will mean they have questions about people they see who look or act differently than them. Instead of correcting them for asking questions, we can provide them with honest, but age-appropriate information. We can help children look for the strengths of the people around them. We can encourage them to look for ways to include others.

A great way to introduce children to human diversity is through stories like the one in this book. I hope that you will read this book to your children, or groups of children that you teach. When you do, try leading a follow-up activity where you identify the ways you are alike and different from each other. Help them see that we are all more alike than we are different, but it can be the differences that make life fun and interesting!

Warmly,
Torrie Dunlap
Chief Executive Officer
Kids Included Together
www.kit.org

Hi, I'm Will, and this is my friend Jake.

Some things about us are the same.
Some things about us are different.

I have brown eyes and blond hair.
Jake has blue eyes and brown hair.

We both like to ride our bikes.

We both like to laugh and tell jokes.

We both like cartoons.

We both like to play at the park.

We both like ice cream, and we both like dogs.

Jake is really good at swimming.

I cheer him on.

I am not very good at swimming,
but Jake helps me and encourages me.

I am really good at video games. Jake cheers me on.

Jake is not very good at video games, but I help him and encourage him.

We help each other, because that's what friends do.

When I grow up, I want to be a firefighter.

Jake thinks I will do a good job and help people.

When Jake grows up, he wants to be a chef.

I know he will do a great job making yummy food.

Jake has Down syndrome. That just means he has an extra chromosome. Everyone has teeny tiny chromosomes in their bodies. You have lots of chromosomes that you can't even see, they are what makes you, you!

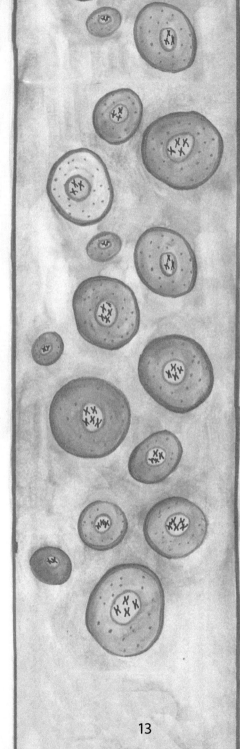

When you are growing inside your mommy, your chromosomes help decide what colour hair you will have, what colour eyes you will have, what your body and brain will be like.

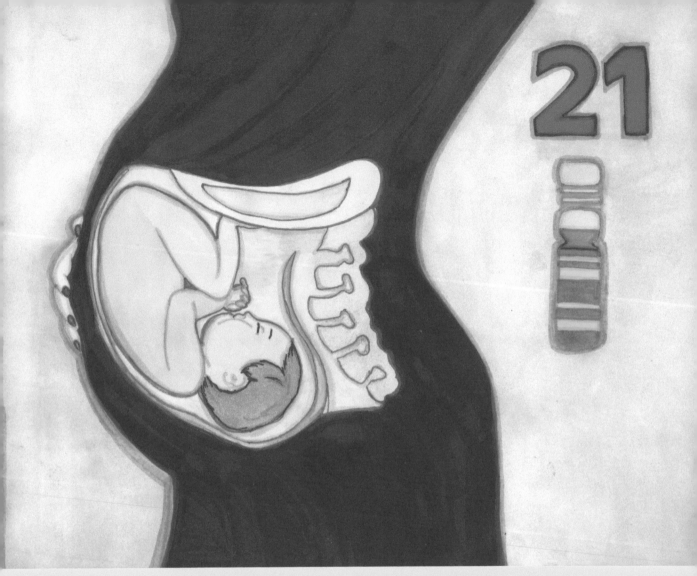

When Jake was growing inside his mommy's body, he got another copy of chromosome number 21. He has more than most people. It doesn't matter to me how many chromosomes Jake has, he's my friend.

Jake has nice almond shaped eyes, they sparkle when he laughs! Most people with Down syndrome have nice almond shaped eyes. Some of them have smaller noses, too, but not all of them.

Some people with Down syndrome may have heart problems, or may need to see the doctor a lot, but not all of them.

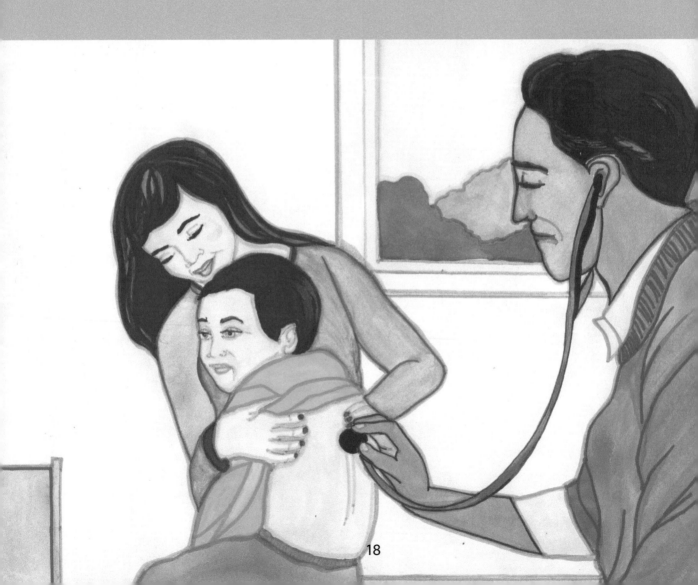

18

Some people with Down syndrome may need glasses or hearing aids, but not all of them.

I know people without Down syndrome sometimes have glasses or hearing aids also.

People with Down syndrome are a little bit different than me, but they are different from each other too! We are all different, but I like it that way. Things would be boring if we were all the same!

Some other things are different about us because of the extra chromosome. Jake took a longer time learning to walk and talk when he was little, but that's okay, he runs fast and talks with me lots now!

Sometimes it takes Jake longer to learn new things at school. He gets extra help with reading, writing and math. The teacher is good at finding different ways to help Jake learn best.

I don't mind that Jake learns some things slower, I am patient, just like he is patient with me. We both agree though that gym time and snack time are the best at school!

Most people really like Jake because he is so fun to be around, but some people make fun of Jake because of the way that he is different. Sometimes they call him names, or don't let him play.

It makes me so sad, and it makes me angry. It is never okay to tease or bully! If those kids would give Jake a chance they would see what a great friend he is!

I am so lucky to have Jake as my friend, he always makes me smile and laugh. He is such a good friend to me, I try hard to always be a good friend to him too! That's what friends do. We are best buds forever!

Thank you for inspiring the adults around you!

Pippa
McIver

Kitaro
Fujii-Purdon

Austin
Lawrence

Logan
Graham

Thank you!

Much thanks and love to the Homies' parents, Andrea Purdon, Miranda and Colin Graham, Caitlin and Tyson McIver, and Alicia and Ryan Lawrence.

Thank you to Jenny Raspberry the Infant & Child Development Coordinator, and to the Board of Community Living Kincardine and District as well as the Executive Director and Assistant Executive Director, for believing in this book.

Thank you to Torrie Dunlap, CEO of KIT – Kids Included Together, inclusion specialists for writing our note to readers, and for supporting this dream.

www.kit.org

Thank you to Ellie Sipila from Move to the Write Editing, Book Design and Digital Production for some sage advice and wisdom.

movetothewrite.com

Thank you to Sarah Diebel our illustrator extraordinaire who put so much time and effort, as well as heart and soul, into this project.

Thank you to Shandra Robbescheuten, our photographer from exquisiteexposure.ca

Thank you to the community of Kincardine Ontario, for the love and support

COMMUNITY LIVING
Kincardine and District
Inspiring Possibilities

Contact us at Community Living Kincardine and District

Telephone: 519-396-9434
Facsimile: 519-396-4514
Email: clkd@tnt21.com
Website: www.clkd.ca

Facebook: Community Living Kincardine and District
Twitter: @CL_Kincardine
YouTube: CommLivingKincardine
Pinterest: CLKD Infant & Child Development pinterest.com/cinfant

CPSIA information can be obtained
at www.ICGtesting.com
Printed in the USA
LVHW070119280119
605462LV00015B/522/P